ElderBerry Wine

Written by **Angela Drew**

Illustrated by **Stephanie Hider**

Written by Angela Drew
Illustrations by Stephanie Hider
Book Design by Praise Saflor

ISBN: 978-1-7372648-1-1 (Hardcover)
       978-1-7372648-2-8 (Softcover)
       978-1-7372648-3-5 (E-Book)
       978-1-7372648-8-0 (Audio Book)

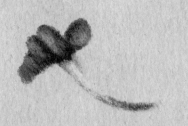

In loving memory of Louis Bland, Jr;
from Elder to Ancestor, August 2021.

Fly high among the ancestors my brother;
they needed you to guide from above.
Your work down here is done.

Time,
time,

oh, the wondrous gift of time.

Everyone gets
the same amount,
your, theirs, mine.

Time,
time,
tell me,
what do you do with time?

I sing and read
and laugh and play,
I smell the flowers every day,
I wish on stars,
I dream,
I pray,
and
make the most
of time.

Time,
time,

they say some things
get better with time...
like cheese
and trees,
and cinnamon teas
and ElderBerry Wine.

Our Elders
aged with grace and strength
their **lives** have **depth**,
and breadth and length,
their **stories alive**
with how their days were spent,
that's ElderBerry Wine.

ElderBerry Wine sounds sweet,
how sweet is ElderBerry Wine?

It's bitter, it's sweet,
it's rich, it's deep,
it's bubbly full
a taste complete,
it breathes and knows,
and sings to sleep,
that's ElderBerry Wine.

ElderBerry Wine
sounds warm,
how warm
is ElderBerry Wine?

Hmmm... well, let me think!
It's Grandma's hands
and songs of love,
it's Grandpa's boots
and too big gloves,
strong arms that hold
just tight enough,
so warm is ElderBerry Wine.

ElderBerry Wine sounds blue...
what color is ElderBerry Wine?

Its purple, it's black,
it's red, its white,
it's light, it's dark,
it's dim, it's bright,
it's rainbow shaded
pure delight,
sublime
is ElderBerry Wine.

ElderBerry Wine seems strong!
How strong is ElderBerry Wine?
It stands up tall
in times of strife,
supports us all,
gives love, gives life.

Robust and bold
through days of old,
foundation of
our family's love.
A chin held high,
big dreams,
big sky,
that's ElderBerry Wine.

ElderBerry Wine,
who makes this ElderBerry Wine?

Well, Elders of course,
the ones we love,
some here on Earth,
some up above...

Like Great-Grandmas Frances and Annie Mae,
purposeful prayers, kind words to say.
Great-grandpa Willie and NaNa Debbie June,
Great-grandma Hiroko, Grandpa Eddie Roy too!
Little Granny Sharon, Grandpa Ronnie, Aunt Betty, Big T,
Auntie Ava, Aunt Cheryl, Aunt Cathy, let's see...

Aunt Tina, Aunt Gina,
Aunt Eleanor, oh my!
Uncle Michael, Uncle Darrell,
Uncles Willie & Walter
on high,
Aunt Jenny, Aunt Penny,
the sweetest
on the planet
Aunt Duchess,
Aunt PeeWee, Uncle Van
and Aunt Janet.

Their love unconditional,
vibrant and true,
respect we must give them,
because it is due.

They share with us wisdom,
they know us so well,
they guide and they teach
with the stories they tell.

They're yours and they're mine,
so proud and so fine,
produced,
regal juice
from one
single long vine,

entangled,
intertwined,
completely
divine,
oh my how I
love me
some
ELder
Berry
Wine

Angela Mason-Drew is a mother, dancer, poet, spoken word performer and self-proclaimed linguistic artist who has loved the rhythm and sounds of words for as long as she can remember. Born in Berkeley, CA, she began writing at age 8 and has always understood that words have the power to soothe, stir, or solidify connection. Her lifelong love affair with storytelling began in the sandbox of her childhood playground and she has played with the magic of words ever since. Angela is a graduate of Holy Names University in Oakland, CA, where she graduated magna cum laude. She is a proud Bay Area native and shares stories from her current home in the Central Valley.

To learn more about Angela and her word artistry, visit her on @she_spits_fire @Angela Drew (Angela Mason) and online at www.linguisticartistry.com

Made in the USA
Las Vegas, NV
24 January 2024